Look
out for
all the
GOBLINS
books:

To Callum
    Happy 9th Birthday,
Lots of love
    Pippa, Paul, Izzy,
Elliot, Anna and
                Katie-mae
                xx xx xx xx

ghost
GOBLINS

David Melling

Hodder
Children's
Books

A division of Hachette Children's Books

A Catalogue record for this book is available from the British Library.

ISBN 978 0 340 94412 7 (HB)
ISBN 978 0 340 93052 6 (PB)

Printed and bound in Great Britain by Clays Ltd, St Ives plc

The paper and board used in this book are natural recyclable products
made from wood grown in sustainable forests.

Hodder Children's Books
A division of Hachette Children's Books
338 Euston Road, London NW1 3BH
An Hachette UK Company

www.hachette.co.uk

Fingerprints by Monika and Luka Melling

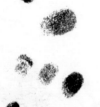

To Elliot Wright and his family

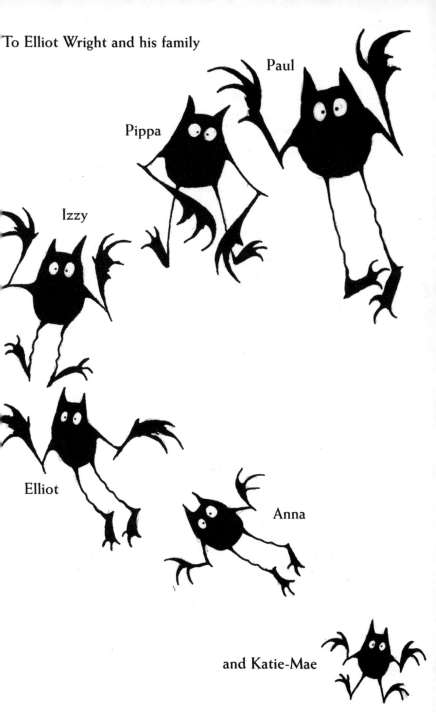

Paul

Pippa

Izzy

Elliot

Anna

and Katie-Mae

The Graveyard

stone goblins

The Bone Collector's Grave

N
W E
S

I magine what it must feel like to be a ghost! Um, wafty and a bit see-through, I guess. I think I'd try to run away and be something else. Only, of course, you can't! Once a ghost, always a ghost. But who tells you how to be a ghost? You know, all the spooky, moaning, chain-rattling stuff. I mean, I suppose that's fun. And just where do you go to sleep at night...?

Introducing the
Ghost Goblins

Gusset

A sensible, practical goblin. She loves knitting
and discovers that, as a ghost, the "wool" is made
of cobwebs.

All ghosts have feet but they don't all choose to
use them – too much to carry
when they're floating
around, I suppose.
Gusset only uses her
feet sometimes.
Legs are
even less
important!

Drysniff

Easily annoyed and sniffs his
disapproval, hence the name.
Gets huffy if you blink too
loud. He's really very cross
about being a ghost!

Sludge

Sludge by name, sludge
by nature. Can't get the
hang of the chain-rattling,
which can be upsetting.
Would prefer to have
wings like the pig.

Other Ghosts

The Flying Pig

She is responsible for the
goblins becoming ghosts. The
shock was enough to make her
a ghost too! Unable to speak
Goblinese, she does her best
with a handful of "oinks" and
some vigorous flapping.

Cold Jack

Also known as *The Collector*. He
was once a goblin, although it was
so long ago he can't remember
what type. He sleeps in the
graveyard and, when called upon,
will meet and introduce new
ghosts to the Afterlife. Struggles
with the cold weather - it affects
his "tubes".

Nightwatch Beetles

Ghost Beetles! They make sure everything in the Afterlife is running smoothly. Any problems and they scuttle around delivering messages (ghost post), offering help where they can.

The Bone Collector

A spooky female Ghost Troll who likes to keep the graveyard tidy, picking up old and forgotten bones which she carries around in various parts of her coat as well as a sack. She makes great Bone Soup!

The Windy Nibblers

A naughty band of Werebats. (Three members so far.)
They can change their shape like shivering shadows!

Butt-knuckle

He's the one in charge
and he gets to wear the
pants. Has false teeth after a
nasty gumming incident which he
doesn't like to talk about.

Armpit

Always bickering with the
others. Grumpy because he
wants to wear the pants.

Hollowsocket

She is the quiet one in the
gang, but can be a right
gummer when she wants to!

Gumming: To suck (or nibble) a leg or arm, while flapping their elbows/wings at the same time (the windy part).

Technique:

1 Remove false teeth

2 Select victim "part"

3 Wind and Nibble!

A FEW FACTS ABOUT GHOST GOBLINS

HABITS AND HABITAT

Ghost Goblins spend their early years in the Moantains – a dark place where the sleeping souls of the "recently snuffed" lie. Resting…waiting…

Cold Jack lives in the graveyard. His coffin has a mind of its own: a sensitive creature with sensitive feelings - wooden ones mostly.

The Stone Giant

Over thousands of years the remains of a giant
were buried up to its neck, eventually turning to
stone. Tunnel Goblins carved stairs that led deep
inside the stone body, creating an enormous
underground tummy cave. Today, it is the home
of ghosts.

A FEW GHOSTING TIPS

How to pass through a solid object
ALWAYS keep your eyes closed until you come out the other side. If you do open them you will find yourself stuck like that for ever. Here are three examples of ghosts with object-sticking problems!

How to remove your head

a) Get a friend to pull your head off

b) Hold your breath so nothing falls out

c) Bring a bucket in case something does.

How to rattle your chains

Think "scary thoughts" while you shake them about or you'll sound like a Christmas jingle, which is just rubbish for haunting.

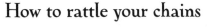

A CLOSER LOOK AT COLD JACK

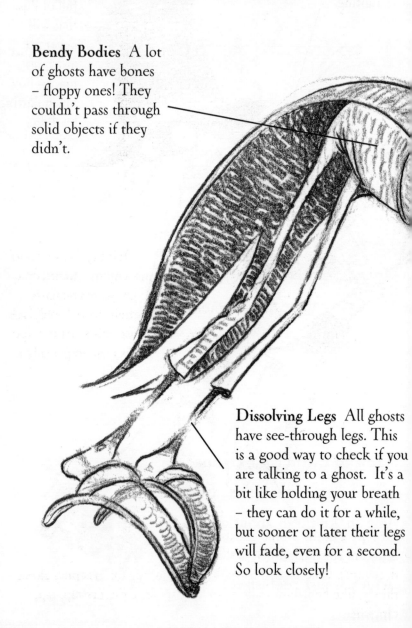

Bendy Bodies A lot of ghosts have bones – floppy ones! They couldn't pass through solid objects if they didn't.

Dissolving Legs All ghosts have see-through legs. This is a good way to check if you are talking to a ghost. It's a bit like holding your breath – they can do it for a while, but sooner or later their legs will fade, even for a second. So look closely!

Cobweb Hair Bonus spooky feature when out haunting.

Crumpled Hat which is full of dust that will never go away, no matter how much patting he does.

Dribbly Nose Cold weather can affect a ghost, particularly their nose. Cold Jack uses his scarf to wipe his nose, especially in a cold fog.

Creepy Hands Some ghosts have different sized hands (or is that my drawing?). One is used for poking, the other for creeping along things, like bedroom walls, with long spidery fingers tap, tap, tapping.

Contents

The Story Begins ...

A bone-white moon glared down at an old graveyard, flashing at the shadows. It lit up a small clump of headstones. They looked tired, leaning against each other like a mouthful of crumbling teeth. The shadows flickered to life and slithered away from the light, some melting into a dark gash in the ground. In the open grave, a coffin shivered!

The lid twitched open and long, bony fingers felt their way, spider-like, around the rim of the coffin, *tap, tap, tapping*. A crumpled figure rose slowly. After a moment's search he pulled out a top hat and clamped it down on his head, releasing a cloud of white dust.

Cold Jack sniffed the air.

He nodded.

1

Yes, it was time, he could sense it.

As he lifted himself out, bones creaking with the effort, thin strands of long, white hair floated like cobwebs around his shoulders. They tickled his nose and made him sneeze into his scarf. After a good blow he pulled it tight around his neck and squinted at the gathering fog. He groaned. Fog was a real nose dribbler, he thought.

Still, duty called. It was time … to *collect*.

Chapter One

Pig-Pats!

Three goblins hurried along by a thin brook that trickled as best it could. It doesn't matter what *kind* of goblins these were, scuttling around in the dark, because they weren't going to be goblins for very much longer. Well, not really.

Gusset was the closest the trio had to a leader. She was a tubby goblin who always had a set of

knitting needles tucked somewhere underneath the heavy cloth of her dress. Good for poking!

The second goblin was called Drysniff. He was impatient and worryingly easy to upset. If anything went wrong, he would blame anyone but himself. And of course, being a goblin, well – things always go wrong. *Always!*

Finally, there was Sludge. There are many words to describe Sludge. Here are just a few of them: clot-mudger, dunder-head, brain-dribbling buffoon (you get the idea). Now if you scoop all those words up in your hands and give them a good old shake, you end up with one big fat word that best describes this idiot: plonker!

All three goblins hopped over the brook and scrambled under a low wooden fence into a muddy field.

"C'mon you two," said Gusset. "We gotta be

in and out, quick as a sticks. Let's start fillin' them buckets with pig-pats. If we don't get a move on, them pigs will be wakin' up, and then we'll be in a right ol' mess."

Drysniff rolled his eyes and mumbled to Sludge, "Nag, nag, nag."

They took out their trowels and started to shovel.

"Can't see a fing in this fog," grumbled Sludge after a few minutes.

"Well, *you* don't need to do no lookin' for no pig-pats," said Drysniff, "'cos you got your feet in some now, you plonker!"

"Aww, that's just rubbish," whined Sludge. He lifted a foot and tried wiping it clean on Drysniff. A bucket bounced off his head and he enjoyed a few quiet moments to himself face down in the mud.

"Will you two burping wind-bags pipe down!"

hissed Gusset, waving her knitting needles irritably.

"Aw, shuddup!" said Drysniff. "You worry too much."

But Gusset was right to worry. They were in a field of sleeping pigs and Gusset knew that pigs will eat *anything*. Pigs have poor eyesight but they've got a good nose on them. They could

snout them out and wolf them down. The trick, thought Gusset, was to make sure you weren't anywhere near one, whether they were hungry or not.

Too late.

"Oh *nuts,*" said Gusset. A dozy pig had suddenly loomed up out of the fog.

It wasn't hungry. It just fancied a sit-down.

In their last moments on this earth, all three goblins took a moment to look up and wonder at just how big and round and pink a pig's bottom really was. And the more they looked, the bigger it got.

And that ... **splat***!* ... was that!

Chapter Two

Cold Jack

"Phew!"

Gusset patted herself, checking for any loose bits. "For a minute, I thought we were all goners!" she said, getting to her feet stiffly and dusting herself down.

"Me too," said Drysniff.

Sludge raised a finger. "Er …!" he said, but the others weren't listening.

"I mean, did you see the size of them buttocks?" continued Gusset.

"Aye! Bound to give you a head-jumble, them wobblers, and no mistake." Drysniff chuckled and turned to Sludge. He stopped smiling.

"What's wrong with you?"

"I feel all … floaty," said Sludge.

"*Floaty?* What d'you mean, floaty?"

"Well, y'know, all up in the air, um … like that pig."

"Pig?" said Drysniff.

Sludge pointed.

Drysniff's jaw dropped.

"Blimey."

"Hot-bone-soup, you're *right!*" cried Gusset,. "It's a flip-flappin' pig!"

Sure enough, the pig that only moments ago had been looming down on the goblins was now floating around their heads like a giant pink balloon. She had a fine pair of white feathered wings that rose high on her shoulders, and she beat them furiously the same way someone might try

swimming for the first time.

Gusset looked down at her slippers. They were empty! Her legs were also missing. And that wasn't all.

Drysniff looked at her. "What's the matter with you? Look like you seen a ghost."

Gusset swallowed. She didn't like the way this was going. She pointed.

He looked down and squealed. "I'm see-through!" His whole body flickered like an old light bulb.

"Yep," said Sludge, "I'm definitely floaty."

"Oink!" said the pig. She still had all four trotters and was quite happy with the new wings.

"Have you noticed the way our voices have changed?" said Gusset.

Drysniff grunted. "Like an echo. You know, as if we had buckets on our heads."

"And look at our clothes, they're all ragged at the edges." said Sludge.

"What are you trying to say?" asked Drysniff.

Before Gusset could reply they were interrupted by an eerie sound. A sound like no other. A sound not of this world! All three goblins had the proper trembles! It started at the top of their heads, shivered down their backs, wobbled in their boots for a while, then scuttled all the way back up again.

They tipped their heads to one side as a squeaking coffin, balancing on four tiny wheels, slowly appeared. It wobbled uncomfortably towards them until two wheels *pinged*, giving the coffin little choice but to sag unhappily to a halt. If coffins could look embarrassed, this coffin would have done.

Something inside fumbled at the handle. They could hear some muttering, more fumbles and, eventually, with a creak the lid flipped open and out stepped …

The goblins gasped.

Cold Jack showed them his teeth, it was his way of smiling, but then he spoilt the effect by suddenly honking loudly into his scarf.

"Ooo, me tubes," he snuffled. "This wretched damp air does nuffin' for me tubes. Blocks 'em up, good and proper."

The goblins watched him adjust his top hat. Then he started to pat himself all over in an effort to rid himself of some of the wrinkles in his clothes. And with every pat he sent up a fresh cloud of dust so that, mingling with the surrounding fog, he briefly disappeared. The dust was part of him and was a constant fuzz that hung around his hat.

"Aha!" he said, reappearing again. "Cold Jack is what they call me! Welcome aboard my *Wailing Wardrobe of Misery*!"

13

Chapter Three

Snuffed Out

Cold Jack couldn't help but notice all three goblins looking at him with their mouths open. He tried to put them at their ease.

"Don't worry about the *Wailing Wardrobe of Misery* – it's just a silly old coffin, actually!" He noticed that this new information didn't seem to be helping. "Of course, I *say* coffin, but really, try thinking of it as a bus."

Still the funny looks, he thought. "Anyone for a ride?" he tried.

He tipped his hat and folded at the middle, which was his way of bowing. When he tried to straighten, there was a series of clicks. "Ooo, me bones," he sniffed. "Ruddy damp, does nuffin' for me bones."

The goblins couldn't quite believe their eyes.

Drysniff found his voice. "T-T-That y-y-yours, then?" he asked.

"It is, as you say, *mine*, yes," smiled Cold Jack, patting the coffin again.

"Ah. Um, I mean … well, why are you c-c-carrying it around?" Drysniff was worried Cold Jack might suddenly open it up and bring out three goblin-sized coffins.

Cold Jack was pleased at last to have a chance to answer a question. He coughed and threw back his shoulders. "My role here today is to welcome you to the Afterlife!"

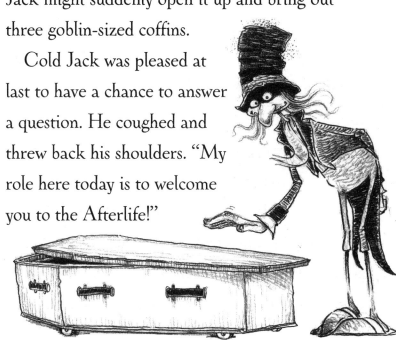

"The *Afterlife?*" said the goblins together.

"You mean we **snuffed it**?" said Drysniff, stealing a glance at Gusset.

"Oh *yes*," Cold Jack said, using that weird grin of his. "You've snuffed it, puffed it – had all the air let out of you, like a flat tyre!"

"*What?* We been and gone and snuffed it because of her?" said Drysniff, jabbing an angry finger in the pig's direction.

"Oink?"

"That would be, *yes!*" said Cold Jack.

"Well, how come the pig is here too?"

"Oink?"

Cold Jack looked at the pig. "Another *excellent* question," he

said, a little too brightly for Drysniff's liking. "Well, this big old lady was so surprised to find three flat goblins stuck to her bottom that her heart jumped up and down for a bit, then it stopped. So she snuffed it too!"

"Then how come she's got wings?" said Sludge. He rather fancied having a go at flying. "Snot fair, *I* want wings!"

Cold Jack grinned. It was a grin dipped in ice. "It doesn't work like that, I'm afraid. You will find different creatures have different, shall we say, 'skills' when they *snuff* it. With pigs, it's mostly wings!"

"Not as big as she used to be either," sneered Drysniff.

"Indeed so," said Cold Jack. "That happens sometimes; small things get big, big things get small. I mean, look at the size of my hands. Whoppers eh?"

"What do we get then?" asked Sludge, who was still thinking about the wings.

"Well, why not step right on in to my office here and find out!" The way Cold Jack spoke, in a cool, calm voice, made everyone feel that it was absolutely the right thing to do. So without any further questions they walked over to the coffin and took a peek.

"Uh, uh!" he said, wagging a long bony finger. "You won't see anything unless you climb *inside*!"

They had the uncomfortable feeling they had no choice … and that once they were inside there would be no turning back.

18

A Coffin Ride

"Chains?" said Sludge. "We get chains? That is just **SO** unfair. I want wings, don't see why not—" He stopped when he saw Cold Jack's face.

"My dear fellow, you must understand, it is not for me to decide. These things just happen." Cold Jack looked all around him then leaned in. Gusset caught a whiff of lemon soap. "Do you think I want all this dust on me?" he said. "Soon as I shake it off, there's more. It don't never go away! Awful business all around but that's how it works, I'm afraid. You get what you're given, and that's that!"

The coffin was surprisingly deep. Frost had

formed on every surface, an unpleasant frozen yellow crust. The goblins lined themselves down the length of the coffin, hovering above three piles of chains. Among these chains were locks and keys and handcuffs, all coiled like sleeping snakes beneath them.

The goblins noticed, now they were inside, that the coffin was transparent! And, despite the open lid, it was pitch black, except for a light that seemed to be coming from the goblins' own bodies.

With a *clinkety-clankety-clunk* the goblins set about draping themselves with chains, like tinsel on a Christmas tree. Eventually they fell back on to the floor of the coffin and watched Cold Jack fit a leash to the pig and hook it to the back end of the coffin.

"She's too big to fit inside with you lot," he grinned. "We'd never get the lid on! But I must say she's doing a grand job with those wings, a real natural. She'll be fine just floating along behind us."

"Oink!" said the pig.

Drysniff smacked a look at the pig. All this was all her fault, he thought miserably.

"Now then," said Cold Jack with a frown, "let me take a quick look at those wheels. Be with you in a tick!"

It gave the goblins a moment to think about what was happening – something they didn't really want to do. They sat there humming stiffly and trying to think happy thoughts.

For the most part they
were successful. All, that is, except
Drysniff. He was getting very uptight about the
glowing. And the floating. So he thought he'd try
something. He stood up and swung a fist at
Sludge. He was hoping it would knock him
flying, but watched his hand pass right through
his head with a lonely *swish*.

"Tickles!" giggled Sludge.

Drysniff sat down, put his head in his hands and moaned.

"That's good," said Cold Jack, popping up suddenly and climbing into the front seat, "but try a touch more volume. And of course you'll need to give those chains a good old shake. Still, not to worry, you'll soon get the hang of it." He sneezed again, sprinkling more dust.

Gusset raised a finger. "My chains keep sliding off!" she said.

"Really? Well, if they don't want to stay on you, they won't!" said Cold Jack with a wink. "Aren't you the lucky one!"

Gusset smiled. "By the way," she said, "who's driving this thing?"

Cold Jack shrugged. "It just … *goes*! That happens a lot here, you'll see! The trick is, when you want to do something, you just *think* about doing it … and most of the time it works!"

The rest of the journey was smothered in silence, except for the squeaking of the coffin wheels. Cold Jack had managed to stick them back on with a couple of slugs.

The Stone Giant

Eventually the coffin lurched to a halt. It was quite sudden and took everyone by surprise, leaving them all crumpled up at one end of the coffin. Cold Jack climbed out and waited patiently whilst the goblins pulled out various fingers and toes from ears and noses, not necessarily their own. There was much grumbling:

"Ow! Don't you ever cut your nails?"

"What IS that? Eewwww, earwax – here, YOU have it!"

"Oink!"

"Wipe that on me and this foot is going up your nose!"

"Oink!"

"Hang on, that's not earwax. It's wet and drippy, **wet and drippy**, I tell you!"

"GET-ME-OUT-OF-HERE!"

There was a loud pop and a single goblin came skidding out of the coffin, landing at the feet of Cold Jack, swiftly joined by two more.

They found themselves standing in the shadow of the tallest mountain they had ever seen. The goblins felt it staring down at them with cruel invisible eyes. They shivered in their boots. The pig, on the other hand, was just happy to be untied from the coffin. All the better to stretch her wings and have a little flap.

"We'll have to walk the last bit," said Cold Jack. "Follow me." His white cobweb hair waved gently in a wind that wasn't there. He led the way, the coffin keeping pace beside him. Gusset tried to work out how it was doing that on its own, but after a while decided she didn't want to know.

They followed a thin crumbling path that wrapped itself loosely around the mountain like a tired old belt. They soon left behind them the few shrubs that had kept them company, and all other signs of life until, at last, they came to the cave. It yawned at them, a terrible mouth frozen in time.

"I've brought you to the Land of *Moan*tains! A place not so popular with creatures from the world of the living," announced Cold Jack.

"You're not kidding," mumbled Sludge grimly.

"This land, indeed these mountains, are built up of from the Souls of Creatures Past. This is an excellent place for beginners like you to learn the craft of ghosting!"

"Looks like a face, does that," said Sludge, stepping back and squinting at a large bulbous rock jutting out. "I can see right up its hooter!"

"That's because it *is* a face!" said Cold Jack, delighted with the observation. "Well, *was* a face."

The goblins shuffled uneasily.

"This is your new home!" said Cold Jack.

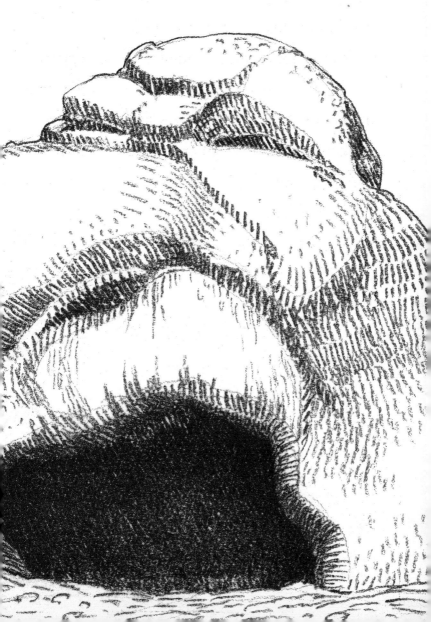

Drysniff coughed. "You mean we're gonna live inside someone's face?"

"Well," said Cold Jack, "not so much the face as the whole body really! Here. Let me explain. You see, this fella used to be a giant. The rest of him is buried inside this mountain. In fact, most of this mountain was once a giant. Only now he's moved on, and what's left is all stone and draughty corridors – you'll love it!"

Drysniff was about to complain about how unfair this whole Afterlife was, when a gust of wind belched out of the cave. It passed through them, ruffling the parts of the ghosts that could still ruffle, and left them all with the feeling that someone had just spoken to them across the vast empty space of time. Drysniff thought he could hear the words singing and dancing on the very air around them:

"Oops, pardon me, I needed that!"

He frowned but said nothing.

"I've brought you here," said Cold Jack, in that polite but chilly tone of his, "so that you can get to know this place. Live here for a while. Understand what you are, and what you can do. You are all **ghosts** now. Enjoy yourselves!"

He opened the lid of the coffin and folded himself inside. His voice was muffled as the lid was lowered. "Don't worry, I'll pop by from time to time, see how you're all doing."

Any final doubts the goblins had had about being ghosts disappeared as they watched Cold Jack's coffin slowly dissolve into the fog.

Chapter
Six

A Bump in the Night

"Y ou go first!"

"Why me?"

"Because you're nearest and my ear hurts."

"Your nose will start hurting in a minute if you keep shoving me like that!"

"Will you two plonks get a move on? It's cold out here."

Two rats, not used to the sound of bickering goblins, stopped gnawing the bone they were sharing and took a moment to watch.

"Actually, it isn't as bad as you think," said Sludge, sniffing the air cheerfully. "Green cheese, I think."

"Should it be raining inside?" said Drysniff

holding out a hand.
"Only, I'm getting
wet."

"First time
I've come
across Indoor
Rain, I'll admit," said Gusset. "At least I *think*
it's rain."

The three goblins edged themselves further
inside. The pig bobbed along happily, rubbing her
pink ghostly back against the rough ceiling of the
cave, which, at that height, helped to light up the
darker corners.

"Ergh!" said Gusset. "These walls are warm!"

"What's this here? I found something!"

"Oi, let go of that or I'll give you such a boot!"

The glow of their bodies was enough for them
to see a line of ragged teeth. It was not, however,
enough to see the stairs …

33

"WHAAAAAAAAAAAAAAARRGGHH!"

BUMP ...

BUMP ...

BUMP ...

BUMPITY ...

BUMP!

34

"I think I've broken something off!" moaned Sludge.

"You couldn't have – we're ghosts, remember?" said Drysniff.

"Then what's this hairy thing?"

"Never you mind!" snapped Gusset. There was a private rustle in the darkness.

"But how come we fell? Aren't we supposed to float?"

"Well," said Gusset, "remember what Cold Jack told us? If we want to *do* something we have to *think* about doing it, and it *should* happen."

"Oink!" said the pig.

"Has anyone noticed what we're sitting in?" asked Drysniff unhappily.

Sludge licked a finger. "It tastes green!"

They got to their feet, formed a line in the slime, and held hands. The pig floated over for a closer look.

"Right then," said Gusset, "let's close our eyes and think about floating." All three screwed up their eyes with the effort.

"Oink! Oink!"

They opened their eyes and, to their surprise, found that they had joined the pig in the air.

They panicked and tumbled once again to the ground.

"Needs practice," said Gusset cheerfully, "but at least we know it works!"

The room, which had been unexpectedly warm when they bundled down the stairs, suddenly grew colder. Something swished past Drysniff's head.

"What was that?" he said.

They held their breath a moment but nothing else happened.

"It's probably rats or something," said Gusset, gripping her knitting needles.

"What, flying rats?" hissed Drysniff.

"Why not? We've got ourselves a flying pig! Now come on, let's take a look around."

The cave was more like a room than the mouth upstairs. It had a low ceiling and was much drier. Once again it was uncomfortably hot and stuffy. The first thing they noticed was a jumble of stones and broken sticks which appeared to be an attempt by someone to make a table! Upon it were set three flat-ended sticks and three bowls, one of which had a steaming lump of something in it. Sludge twitched his nose in its direction. His

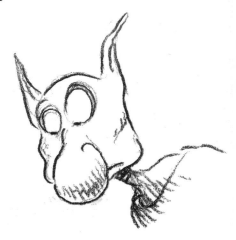

37

nostrils streamed. He gasped and pulled back quickly.

Before he could say anything, the intense heat of the place was suddenly replaced for the second time by an ice-cold sharpness that stung. There came an awful smell, so strong it curled the very hairs on Drysniff's tongue.

"SWISHY-WOO! SWISHY-WOO!"

"I don't know why you p-p-plonks are making silly noises," hissed Gusset. "This is no time to be mucking about."

"That wasn't me!"

"Or me!"

"Well, if it wasn't you two—" Gusset didn't have time to finish.

Suddenly, the air was alive with the fizz and crackle of ghostly shapes. Hooded, winged creatures that snarled and

38

pinched, dipped and nipped!

"SWISHY-SWISHY-SWIRLY-WOO!" they moaned.

The goblins and the pig jumped and clung to each other.

"SHOO! GO AWAY, GO ON, BUZZ-OFF!"

Well, the *swishy-woos* and the *buzz-offs* went on for a while until all the ghosts packed

into that tight little room realized
that they were acting like a silly bunch of
doughnuts.

The screaming hooded creatures that had
attacked the Ghost Goblins fell away, their black
shapes swooping over to a spot in the furthest
corner of the room, where they hung upside
down from the ceiling like bats. In the darkness
the Ghost Goblins heard them whispering
urgently, the whispers turning to chatters and
then hissing.

"You go – go on, I did it last time."

"Only if I get to wear the pants."

"Now I told you before about that – it was my idea so I get first
go!"

"What about Armpit? He's not done it for ages."

"Ooo, you *fibber*! I went the time when them
rabbits came a-hopping down here!"

"That hardly counts, and you know it!"

They stopped, suddenly aware they were being overheard.

There was a bit of shoving and then one of them snapped, "Oh, all *right*, but I'm not using the carrots!"

Small umbrella-wings opened and one of the creatures fluttered to the ground, bouncing several times. It sprang to its feet and hopped awkwardly towards them, floppy as a sock.

It was a curious fuzzy little thing, about half the size of the Ghost Goblins. Two ice-blue eyes glared out of a hooded mask which covered almost half of its small

round body. But the most striking thing about the creature was that it was wearing a large pair of pants. Two trembling legs, thin as string, poked out of the bottom.

The creature came right up to Drysniff and, with a series of loud snorts, started sniffing his knees. "Hmm, goblins, eh? What you lot doing here?" it said.

"That's what we'd like to ask you," said Drysniff.

"Us lot? We're here on account of it being our home – so there!"

"Well, we're here," said Sludge, "'cos we were told we could live here, so ner with bells on!" He tinkled his chains, but he hadn't practised enough yet and it sounded like a holiday jingle.

"Ooo, Christmas," he heard one of creatures whisper.

"Now *listen*," said Drysniff, "we don't know

who you plonkers are, with your sniffy-hooters and your swishy-woos, but you'd better bog off before we give you a right goin' over!"

"We're going nowhere. It's you lot that need to be doing the **shifting**, and take that flying pig with you!"

"That flying pig is one of us!" said Drysniff, surprising himself. Up until now the pig had been the reason they were ghosts and he'd been cross about that.

"Who are you plonks, anyway?" said Gusset.

There was a twitter of irritation from the ceiling shadows.

"They call me Butt-knuckle," said the creature with the pants. He waved a crooked claw. "That's Hollowsocket, and in the corner is Armpit."

"Halloo!"

"Halloo!"

Gusset thought she saw them waving.

"What sort of ghosts are you?" snorted Drysniff.

"Right scary ones," said Butt-knuckle slowly. "Of course, you might know us by another name … for we are …

The Windy Nibblers!"

The Windy Nibblers

"The Windy Wobblers?" said Drysniff.

"*Nibblers*," said Butt-knuckle stiffly, "the Windy Nibblers."

"And what exactly does that mean?"

"That means, watch out or you'll be sorry, that's what!"

Drysniff grinned and took one step forward. "Oh yeah, and who's going to make me? Mr Pants here?"

Butt-knuckle growled and bared his sharp white teeth. To Drysniff's surprise the Windy Nibbler took them out of his mouth and stuffed them into a pant-pocket.

"Pah!" laughed Drysniff, "and what you gonna

do now – give me a gummy nibble?"

"Yeth!" said Butt-knuckle with a lopsided grin. Drysniff was telling himself he should be laughing. False teeth!

But there was something he didn't like about that grin. It had trouble written all over it. He took a step back but it was too late. Butt-knuckle sprang. Drysniff could only look down in horror as Butt-knuckle's mouth opened wider than he thought possible and his pink dribbly gums fastened themselves around his left leg.

Drysniff cried out, kicking as best he could whilst the Windy Nibbler flapped his wings and tightened his grip. Then, with a series of unpleasant sucking noises, he nibbled and gummed and slobbered up and down like a dog chewing a bone.

"Argh! Me leg!" wailed Drysniff.

When Butt-knuckle finally finished, it sounded like a rubber plunger letting go. He sat back and popped his teeth back in. Then he dabbed at the corner of his mouth and smacked his lips. "Hmm, pickled onions, interesting!"

"Look what he's been and gone and done to me leg!" shrieked Drysniff, when he could catch his breath. His leg was bright pink, quite lumpy and very, very wet.

"Ooo!" said Sludge, "that does look sore!"

Gusset took out her knitting needle and gave Butt-knuckle a sharp prod. "You keep them nippy pinchers to yourself."

"Ouch!" said Butt-knuckle, rubbing his arm. "Them needles are sharp!"

"Oh *brilliant!*" gurgled Drysniff. **"Poke him with a knitting needle, *that'll* do it! Can't someone bite his leg off or something?"**

"Anyway, listen," said Butt-knuckle. "It was you lot that started it, coming in here with your tinkly decorations."

"These are not decorations," said Sludge, "these are our *Chains of Horror* – and don't you forget it."

48

"Ha!" said Armpit. "Sound like Christmas bells to me!"

"Don't you listen to him," said Gusset, who knew how upset Sludge was about the chains. "I thought your chains sounded right scary – gave me tummy the wibbles and no mistake."

Sludge looked pleased. "D'you think so? Because to be honest I've been a bit worried I wasn't doing it right. I've been having a right old practice, I have, and I reckon the best way is to—"

"Excuse me!" wailed Drysniff, eyes bulging, "but what about my leg?"

"Yeah, well, sorry about that," said Butt-knuckle, "but like I say, you lot started it. What we need," he continued, "is Cold Jack.

49

He brought us all here."

"I agree," said Gusset. "But how do we go about calling him?"

"That's easy," said Armpit. "Nightwatch Beetles."

"What?" said Sludge. He was feeling a bit peckish and liked the sound of beetles.

"Nightwatch Beetles, they're the messengers around here."

"How long will they take?" snarled Drysniff.

"Cold Jack'll be here by morning, sure of it."

"What we gonna do while we wait?" said Gusset. "I mean, where are we going to stay? Mind if we bunk down here for the night?"

Before the Windy Nibblers could reply Drysniff began gargling again.

"If you think I'm gonna stay in the same place as that leg-sucking-loony, you got another think coming!"

50

Chapter Eight

Nightwatch Beetles

Cold Jack arrived back at his grave in a very bad mood. The wheels of his coffin kept coming off (those slugs were useless), and he'd had to walk the last two miles carrying the wretched thing. The fog had long gone and the ground was now lit up by the grin of a cheerful moon, which he found really annoying.

At last, he heaved the coffin grumpily into the grave and flopped himself inside, releasing yet more dust. He closed the lid on a long and difficult night, took a deep breath and shut his weary eyes.

He was just drifting off into his favourite dream (about talking dust-balls) when there came a series of *taps* on the coffin lid.

Cold Jack groaned. Now ghosts don't use bad words normally – if they want to shock anyone they have more obvious ways of doing it.

But the words that crawled out of Cold Jack's mouth and burrowed their way through the floor of the coffin and down into the cold damp earth were shocking.

"Yoohoo!" Tap, tap, tap. "Mr Cold Jack, sir – you in there?" said a Nightwatch Beetle, named

Munch. "Only we have a problem with your latest 'job' and feel that an error has been made which requires your immediate attention!"

Cold Jack thought about pretending he wasn't there, but he knew they'd only make sure by chewing their way through the side of the coffin. And so they did! Before he could stop them, a dozen holes appeared by his left ear.

"Ah, that's better," said Munch. "Nice bit of wood that, very tasty!"

Cold Jack wrestled with his temper.

"What exactly seems to be the problem?"

"Ah, now then, hmm, that is the question – yes, yes, so it is," said Munch. He was busy filling his pockets with

wood crumbs.
Cold Jack
sighed heavily. A
conversation with a
Nightwatch Beetle took
twice as long as with any other
creature he knew, living or dead.
And Cold Jack had spoken with some very
strange creatures in his time.

"Well, Mr Cold Jack, sir, it has come to my attention, so it has,
yes, yes, that those Ghost Goblins of yours, you know, the ones with
the flying pig, hmmm? Well, the place you took them to in the
Moantains is already occupied by the Windy Nibblers!"

Cold Jack growled. "I'd forgotten I put them
in the Stone Giant as well, blast it!"

"Can we help in any way?"

He rubbed the sleep from his eyes and
yawned. "Don't suppose it could wait for half an
hour? Only it's been a long night and I could *die*

for a quick snooze!"

The beetles clacked their thin black legs against the side of the coffin.

"No, no, no, no, no! Oh, you must come now, so you must. They're making too much noise as it is, arguing and the like. Might wake others – others that don't need waking, yes?"

"Fighting?" asked Cold Jack, his eyes open for the first time during the conversation.

"Yes, yes! Fighting and biting and needle-stick-jousting! Too loud, the screaming is just too loud!"

Cold Jack had heard enough. With a deep sigh he hauled himself out and set off once again, the coffin strapped to his back.

Stick Insects

By the time Cold Jack arrived the ghosts had taken the fight outside. Drysniff had his arms around a Windy Nibbler and was shaking him upside down. Gusset was hopping about with her knitting needles, jabbing at anyone that came too close. Nearby, a pair of twitchy legs poked out from underneath the dozing pig – muffled sounds suggested it was another

 Windy Nibbler. A little way into the shadows Cold Jack could make out Butt-knuckle. He was gumming Sludge and there were screams a-plenty.

Cold Jack filled the air with a thick mist that muffled the screams, preventing them from waking the souls in the surrounding moantains. Then he found a rock to sit on, unscrewed the lid from a jar of pickled stick-insects, took one out and began chewing it thoughtfully. Eventually, as the final screams faded, he got to his feet. The only sound was the occasional toot of escaped air from the Windy Nibbler who was still under the pig.

"Clearly," said Cold Jack, spitting flecks of stick-insect as he spoke, "I have made a mistake. I have given you both the

Stone Giant for your home. It is therefore my decision to hold a Haunting Contest. The winners," he said wiping his nose on a sleeve, "will be allowed to stay here!"

The Heebie-Jeebies

Night sighed heavily, adding to the fog with a cloud of breath that hung in the air like a bad smell. Cold Jack had led the ghosts away from the Land of Moantains altogether. It was better not to disturb those souls that still slept.

When they arrived at the graveyard he took them to the largest and most impressive grave. Ancient carvings of dragons and serpents writhed around the headstone. The Ghost Goblins and the Windy Nibblers sat down while Cold Jack explained the rules.

"Now then," he snuffled, "this competition is simply called **The Heebie-Jeebies** and the

rules are *dead* easy! Basically, you have to scare the living daylights out of anyone that sets foot inside this graveyard!"

The Windy Nibblers grinned their lopsided grins and huddled together, whispering excitedly.

The Ghost Goblins, on the other hand, were not happy.

"We don't even know *what* we can do, never mind *how* we can do it!" mumbled Drysniff to the others. "We don't stand a chance."

Sludge rattled his chains. "I could try bopping this lot over someone's head. May not sound scary when I shake them, but I bet they hurt bouncing off your noggin!"

Gusset sighed. "We've just got to do the best we can with what we know, I suppose."

"Right," said Cold Jack, holding up a fist. "I have in my hand a pickled stick-insect. I believe all you can see are its legs. I need one of you from each team to pull a leg off! Whichever team has the shortest leg will go first!"

Armpit pulled out the winning leg and the Windy Nibblers yelped with joy, dancing and skipping around in circles.

"All right, calm down!" said Cold Jack. "It only means you start first, you haven't won yet!"

He told the Ghost Goblins to sit out of the way in the branches of a nearby tree.

"That's not fair," said Armpit, "if they see us haunting they'll nick our ideas!"

"Don't worry, let them," sniggered Butt-knuckle. "They've got no chance – it'll be something for them to think about when they're out looking for a new home!"

"Now then," said Cold Jack, "we get plenty of visitors to our graveyard every night. We just have to wait for something to come along. Once they step inside the graveyard we start. The Heebie-Jeebies has three simple rules:

"*One:* You have one hour to scare your victim out of the graveyard, any way you can.

"*Two:* The team that scares its victim away in the quickest time is the winner.

"*Three:* Any other rules I'll make up as we go along. Questions, anyone?"

"No," said Butt-knuckle, swiping a look at the Ghost Goblins. **"We're ready to go a-haunting!"**

How to be a Ghost!

The Ghost Goblins turned their backs on the jeers of the Windy Nibblers.

"This is no good," said Gusset, "no good at all. If we are to stand any chance of winning this competition we have to find out exactly what we are capable of doing. We are ghosts after all."

"But how?" asked Drysniff.

Just then they heard a tiny clicking. A Nightwatch Beetle appeared on the grave next to them and introduced himself as Legs-Eleven (although he only had six). He spoke to them in his small quick-fire voice.

"We know all about you and what's happening here tonight. It's our job to try and make things right, to fix things that need fixing. We agree with Cold Jack about holding a competition, yes, yes. That is the fairest way. But what is not fair is that you were never given *The Book*."

He clicked and rubbed his legs and more beetles appeared carrying a small black book.

"Everything you need to know is within those pages – but be quick, yes, yes? You may not have long."

Gusset took the leather-bound book. It smelt of eggs. She asked the pig to fly over and check what the Windy Nibblers were doing. On hearing that they were still waiting for a victim, the goblins all sat down and began to read.

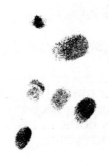

Let us take a quick look at one of the
pages from this book . . .

Haunting Techniques for the Beginner

★

• Chain Rattling

1. Wrap ghost in chains

2. Pick up ghost

3. Shake

ting-a-ling

•Moaning and Groaning

1. Place pin in shoe

2. Walk

•Throwing objects

TIP: Small goblins work best - they don't stick to the walls

Chapter
Twelve

The Victims

The Windy Nibblers hung upside down in the highest arms of the tallest tree they could find. It was still quite foggy so they would need to sharpen their senses to spot anything. It didn't help that they had all been arguing about whose turn it was next to wear the pants.

"Me of course," said Armpit. "I saw them first!'

"Yeah, but it was my idea to put them on!" said Butt-knuckle.

"But that was ages ago. Should be me 'cos I got a bigger bottom."

"Too right there – never seen such wobblers," said Armpit.

This had lasted for ten minutes and it was only after the threat from Cold Jack that if they didn't shut up he would disqualify them that finally they settled into a sulky silence.

Suddenly, Butt-knuckle caught a movement, a rustling in a bush close by. He sniffed the damp chilly air and smiled.

Stone Goblins … of *course*!

There were two of them. On this fateful night they were hunting stones. (No one knows why Stone Goblins do this. All we know is they are just bananas about stones!) They had caught the delicious flinty smell of the graveyard's big fat stones, all surrounded by the smaller stones of the boundary wall. Stone Goblin heaven!

Butt-knuckle narrowed his eyes. The Stone Goblins seemed to have tangled their collecting nets in the bushes. The bushes shook violently for a few moments, then the Stone Goblins were free and running towards the wall. Little did they know that their time in the graveyard was going to be a living nightmare!

With a squeal of excitement the Windy Nibblers looked across at Cold Jack, who was cloaked in the shadow of a nearby tree. He gave them a nod.

The Haunting Contest had begun!

The Ghost Goblins heard the Windy Nibblers and guessed what was happening. Tucking the book into one of her more private pockets,

Gusset led the others back, keen to see if they could learn anything new from the haunting.

They arrived to see two Stone Goblins sniffing a large headstone.

The Windy Nibblers sniggered and fizzled and became part of the fog, reappearing moments later above the Stone Goblins' heads. Hollowsocket was so excited by what they had discovered, she couldn't stop dribbling. For a moment, the Stone Goblins thought it was raining.

Saggypant and Seepage Meet
the Windy Nibblers

The Stone Goblins had just managed to prize
loose the headstone and were giving it a
quick cuddle when Butt-knuckle appeared in front
of them. He was so much a part of the fog that at
first the goblins thought they must be imagining
things.

"*Give … me … my … grave!*" Butt-knuckle
moaned.

Now these Stone Goblins were twin brothers.
Their names were Saggypant and Seepage and if
you've read *Stone Goblins*, you will know just how
clueless these two were. Yes, they could see
something. But right then they had more

74

important things on their mind. Like how they were going to get this lovely stone back to their tunnel.

Butt-knuckle frowned. Perhaps they hadn't heard him, he thought. He tried again.

"I … said … **Give … me … my … grave!**"

But the Stone Goblins were having none of it.

"Get your own blinkin' stone, we saw it first!" said Seepage.

Armpit, sensing Butt-knuckle's frustration, appeared at Saggypant's ankle, chose his spot, and started gumming!

As you have already learned, Stone Goblins

are bonkers for stones. But did you know their bodies were as tough as old stones as well?

Armpit found out just how *un*chewable they really were. He stood up, held out his hand and spat out a mouthful of teeth.

"Perhaps," mumbled Butt-knuckle, "this isn't going to be quite as easy as I thought."

It was Hollowsocket's turn. Bearing down on the goblins she screamed, one wing sprouting claws as she swooped amongst them. She scratched the top of their heads, whilst at the same time trailing behind her a foul smell that could knock out a cow.

"Phew!" chuckled Seepage, waving a hand in

76

front of his nose. "Nice one, Saggs!"

Butt-knuckle swallowed. He watched poor
Hollowsocket fly off in a huff, whilst Armpit was
on all fours looking for a tooth he'd dropped.

He couldn't understand it. He'd come across
Stone Goblins before. They were dead easy to
scare. But these two, he thought. All they cared
about was the stone.

Butt-knuckle clicked his fingers. "I've got it!"
he said.

"Well whatever it is, don't give it to me,"
snapped Armpit. "I got enough problems of my

own. I mean, look at me teeth – took ages to get them as sharp as that!"

"Paf! I wouldn't worry about it, you should try false teeth," said Butt-Knuckle, removing his set and waving them in the air. "Since I've had these bad boys I don't never need to do no cleaning, nor nuffin!" he said cheerily.

"I'm not sure I want to be in this silly competition," whined Hollowsocket. "I tell you, they're just rude!"

"Don't worry, me Nibblers. All those plonkers care about is how great their stone is. We just have to possess it – then we can do the haunting from inside! That'll give them something to think about."

"Hey, might have a point there!" said Armpit. "I reckon if all three of us can fit inside, that'll give them the windy-pops and no mistake!"

Once again they shivered into the fog and

glided towards the Stone Goblins, who had managed to move the headstone some way towards the stone boundary.

Butt-knuckle went first. He closed his eyes and thought hard about stone-crumbs. Then he poured himself into the gravestone, like sand from a bucket. The others followed and together they all became part of the stone.

The goblins, grunting with effort, noticed a change. Something was wrong.

"Blimey, this stone's got cold all of a sudden."

"Sure has, bruv!"

"Let's put it down here for a minute, have a rest." There followed a thump, which took the Windy Nibblers by surprise and Armpit nearly fell out!

"Cor, look at that – it's frozen solid!"

Sure enough the stone had a crackle of ice running right through it.

Just then it shook and trembled and, in perfect unison, three ghastly heads appeared and moaned their terrible moans.

This time it worked. Their happy stone-huggy thoughts popped like a bubble, and at last the Stone Goblins did what was expected of them.

"Whhaaaaaaaarrgghhhhh!"

Saggypant tried to run in four different

directions at once and promptly fell over. He looked up in horror at the sight of Hollowsocket bearing down on him. She was clawing her face, deciding not to scream but to hiss instead. This time she was pleased to see her victim was giving her the full attention she deserved.

Meanwhile, Seepage covered

his eyes and screamed as Armpit welled up out of the stone. The Windy Nibbler grinned his terrible grin, flashing those small pointy teeth. It was still an appalling sight, even though most of them were missing.

But it wasn't over yet for the Stone Goblins. The brothers managed to scramble to their feet, only to be met by a ghastly figure bearing down on them. Butt-knuckle lurched towards them, his evil eyes squinting out from behind his black mask; his terrible lopsided grin; those hideous pants!

The Stone Goblins turned and fled, scrambling over the wall and away into the night. The Windy Nibblers gathered on the wall, feet dangling over the side, and listened with delight to their fading screams.

"Eighteen minutes and fifty-two seconds!" said Cold Jack. "Not bad!"

The Bone Collector

With the growing dawn came the news that the Ghost Goblins had already guessed. They would have to wait until the following night for their turn. Only then would the winner of the competition be known.

"There are plenty of places here for you all to rest up," said Cold Jack.

With that, he yawned, dabbed his nose, wished them all a good day and disappeared below ground, leaving a cloud of dust that hung in the air like a thought bubble. The Ghost Goblins had a lot to think about!

Gusset pointed to a deep open grave almost

entirely hidden by a bank of nettles and shrubs. It was big enough for all four of them. "Let's get bedded down as soon as we can," she said, fingering the black book. "We've got a lot to read about if we want to win."

The others agreed, but no sooner had they arranged themselves as comfortably as they could among the beetles and spiders and other leggy creatures than a shuffling, scratching noise could be heard outside. And even ghosts can be made to jump!

"You hear that?" hissed Drysniff.

Stiff with silence, three goblin faces (the pig had fallen asleep) pushed their way up through the nettles and found themselves looking at a dark figure. It was holding on to something large and heavy-looking – a body, perhaps?

They could hear the figure sniffing the air. It turned slowly, revealing a face covered in a

thick bush of hair.
They gasped – a
female troll!

**"What you
doing in my
bed?"** she
grinned.

The Ghost
Goblins
trembled.

"Y-y-your
b-b-bed?" said
Drysniff.

"Fear not,
dearie, I welcome the
company. Now shove up
and I'll join you!"

The goblins let go of the
brambles and fell back down into

the grave. The sack landed next to them with a clatter, followed by the heavy thump of the troll.

"My name is not so important," she said. "Everyone knows me as the Bone Collector!"

"You collect b-b-bones?" said Drysniff.

The troll cackled. "Well, if I don't, who will? Gotta keep this place tidy!" She pulled the sack towards her and without warning upended the contents. An assortment of bones tumbled out: long ones, short ones, twisted and broken ones! "Now then," she said, "anyone hungry?"

To the goblins' amazement the troll pulled out a handful of twigs from her beard and started a small fire! Before long she had water bubbling in a small black pot.

"I'm guessing," said the troll, "from the look on them faces of yours that you have yet to experience the pleasures of Bone Soup!"

The goblins were lost for words. Not so the Bone Collector.

"I've been watching you from a distance. Well, I never did take to them Windy Nibblers and their gummy ways! Don't like the way they'll suck a bone dry then chuck it over their shoulder. No respect – messy devils! So I reckon it's only right for me to tell you a few haunting tricks of my own."

A wide grin spread across her face, showing more gum than tooth. The goblins noticed the teeth she did have didn't look like they belonged to her. It all looked a bit homemade in there!

They tried not to think about it and settled down to listen … and learn.

Chief Cheesyfeet and
the Stone Goblins Return

As soon as night spread out its thick velvet
cloak, the graveyard came to life! Cold
Jack was already sitting by the dragon grave
and had just finished scratching a few
notes, with freshly squeezed
black-beetle ink, when

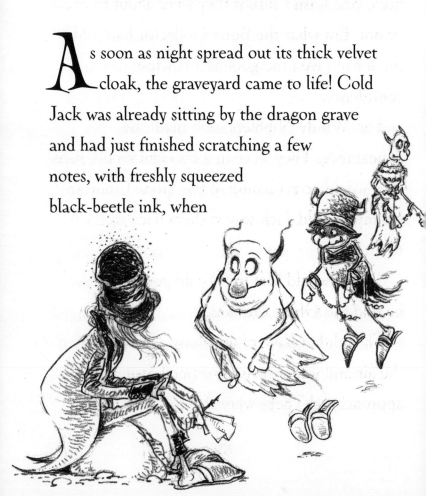

the Ghost Goblins arrived.

"Evening!" He paused, looking at them all carefully. "You seem … well," he said slowly.

"Yes," said Gusset. "We feel well, thank you!" A hot prickle of guilt ran up and down her neck. She wasn't sure if they were about to cheat or not. But what the Bone Collector had told them had given the goblins a newfound confidence.

The Windy Nibblers soon made an appearance. They were in a cheerful mood, sure they would be returning to the Stone Giant in triumph. Cold Jack waved them back to the trees.

"If you would like to take up your position," he told the Ghost Goblins.

They didn't have to wait long. Gusset sniffed the air and was surprised to smell Stone Goblins approaching! There were three of them. One

appeared to be loosely bound on top of a large stone which was being carried by two other goblins who struggled under the weight. It didn't help that the small goblin on top had his arms wrapped around a large stone of his own. Typical Stone Goblins! They made a loud and clumsy entrance and once again, as soon as they landed inside the graveyard, Cold Jack nodded. It was the turn of the Ghost Goblins to go a-haunting!

The Stone Goblins were none other than Chief Cheesyfeet and the hapless brothers Saggypant and Seepage. The chief had been so excited to hear the brothers' tale about a "land of giant stones", he insisted they take him there the very next night. It was just the sort of place he needed to choose a new throne. Saggypant and Seepage's hysterical blabbering about ghosts had fallen on deaf ears.

And now, here they were. Chief Cheesyfeet quivered with excitement. Even Saggypant and Seepage, once their nostrils had caught that sweet smell of stone, had forgotten the more unpleasant details of their visit to the graveyard the previous night.

Their happy state of dreamy befuddlement

didn't last long. A sound of bones clattering broke their concentration. From behind a tree there appeared a skeleton. It moved awkwardly towards them. As it drew nearer they could see it was made up of a very odd collection of bones. It was like no creature they knew!

Following the Bone Collector's instructions, Gusset had spent most of the night creating the skeleton from the troll's sack of bones. She had learned how to knit cobwebs, creating a strong silver thread. Now, she floated above the skeleton, working it like a puppet. The trick, of course, was that both Gusset and the strings were invisible, making it look like a bizarre ghostly creature on the prowl! With claws and fangs and the rattle of the chilly white bones, it was a terrible creature to behold.

The Stone Goblins stared at the thing, terror rippling through their bodies but unable to move.

Gusset wasn't put off by her victims' response. This was only *Phase One!*

Now it was Sludge's turn. He erupted from the grave the Stone Goblins were hugging, screaming with such force that a blast of wind knocked the Stone Goblins over. This certainly

grabbed their attention.
Goggle-eyed, Chief
Cheesyfeet, who had
caught the full blast of
foul air which erupted
from Sludge's
yawning mouth,
spluttered.

"Get rid of that
thing," he cried.
"It's upsetting me
Royal Sniffs!"

He was about to bark
more orders when he caught
the look on the faces of
Saggypant and Seepage.
With bulging eyes they
pointed shaky fingers at their
chief and babbled:

"You got a finger sticking out yer ear!"

Chief Cheesyfeet could hear the words but they made no sense. And then a funny tingling sensation inside his head made him frown, then blink, then giggle. He looked at the brothers again. They were screaming now, and still pointing at him. He decided to join them.

"Whoah! Somethin's movin' about inside my head!" he said.

"You got a long bony finger sticking out your ear holes, Chief!"

Sure enough, Sludge had learned to play Finger

in Your Ear. It was a simple trick and one of the first that all ghosts learned. Sludge was thrilled with the effect!

The Stone Goblins were not.

"I can feel it wigglin'!" wailed Chief Cheesyfeet. "Ooo, ooo, it's ticklin' me brain!" he giggled nervously. "Get it out! Get it out!"

Saggypant and Seepage pulled at the finger as best they could, but it dissolved into smoking ice and with a squeal, they fell over. Sludge decided to floss Chief Cheesyfeet's head for a while, then, rising high into the night air, he looped back down with an ear-piercing scream and a rattle of his chains.

The poor Stone Goblins had had enough and they bolted. Unfortunately for the Ghost Goblins, but to the delight of the Windy Nibblers, they scattered in different directions.

They were running away from the wall and deeper into the graveyard.

And to make things worse, a sudden fog blew up, hiding the Stone Goblins from view.

"Eleven minutes to go!" cheered the Windy Nibblers. "You'll never make it!"

Chapter Sixteen

Tick Tock!

There was a moment of blind panic, then the Ghost Goblins started to track the Stone Goblins' screams through the fog. They found them, eventually. Standing at the foot of a familiar grave, horror on their faces, the Ghost Goblins could make out muffled voices from inside a very familiar coffin.

It was the grave of Cold Jack!

The Ghost Goblins shivered. The dark night suddenly grew darker, the cold air grew colder, and ice began to crackle and spread through the grass around their feet.

"Get … those … persons … out … of … my … home!" said the slow, dangerous voice of Cold Jack.

The Ghost Goblins dropped to their knees (if they had them) and cocked an ear, all the better to hear with! Clearly, the Stone Goblins had no immediate plans to leave.

"Thems were ghosts, that's what thems were!"

"Y-y-yeah! W-w-we'll w-w-wait until m-m-morning.
Then w-w-we'll leg it out of here!"

"Six minutes!" chanted the Windy Nibblers.

Just then, the pig appeared.

"Oink!"

"She's trying to tell us something," said
Sludge.

"Oink! Oink!"

Sure enough, the pig was trying to nudge the
goblins aside. Gusset clicked her fingers.

"I've got it! I'll knit some cobwebs – you
know, the way the Bone Collector showed us.
Then we can tie the coffin to Piggy here, and she
can lift it out of the graveyard. Job done!"

It took precious minutes to organize. The
Ghost Goblins held their breath. "Three
minutes!" cried the Windy Nibblers.

With a grunt and heave the pig flapped
her wings as best she could. Slowly the coffin

moved. More muffled voices from inside.

"What's going on out there?"

"I need the loo!"

The pig strained and pulled and flapped her little piggy wigs and the coffin rose out of the grave.

The Ghost Goblins cheered as the pig made her way towards the gates. But suddenly, there was a "*snap-ping*"! The cobwebs broke and the coffin tilted and crashed to

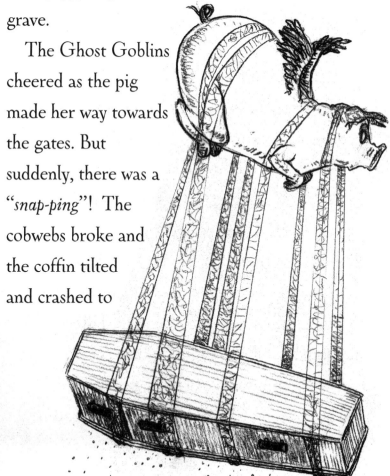

the ground. Somewhere close by, Cold Jack's growl could be heard scratching the night air.

The Windy Nibblers cheered. "Oh, that's done it," they laughed. "You've only got two minutes to go, you'll never make it!"

Gusset looked at the others. All three sighed and bowed their heads. They knew it was too late. They had lost.

"OINK! OINK! OINK!" the pig said, with an urgency the Ghost Goblins had never seen before. Before the goblins could stop her, she brought her large wobblers crashing down on the coffin.

The coffin, after a difficult few nights, gave up. It exploded, sending a shower of matchwood over a large and troubled area. The resulting sound was drowned out by the cry from Cold Jack, **"NOOOOOOOO!"**

The Windy Nibblers cried with laughter and nearly fell out of the tree.

The Stone Goblins found themselves very much the centre of attention. Taking one look at their audience, Chief Cheesyfeet cried, "Leg it!"

They scattered. One did make it through the gap in the wall. But the other two made goblin-shaped holes in the wall itself.

Nothing was going to get in their way.

Cheats?

The Ghost Goblins should have been celebrating, but they could just make out the grey outline of Cold Jack in the fog. He was on his knees, honking loudly into his damp, damp scarf. He cleared away a bit of splintered coffin, slumped back on to the edge of a grave and sighed. Looking down, he noticed something winking at him from under a clump of thistles. He pulled out one of the missing wheels from his coffin. Tears welled up in his eyes.

But after a time he reminded himself it hadn't been the only coffin over the years – there had been others! Only, he had just got it nice and comfy, like a bed you've had for ages. It would take him many years to get a new one to be just as comfortable, with all the right lumps in the all right places. Still, he mused, those wheels were rubbish, so perhaps it wasn't so bad!

The fog began to thin as he took out his clipboard and wrote the winners' names on a crumpled certificate. He returned to the others. Everyone was bickering, but when they saw him they stopped.

"Cold Jack, we're so sorry about your coffin."

"Must be a disqualification, I reckon," said Butt-knuckle, hopping on those stringy legs of his.

Cold Jack held up a hand. He cleared his nose (that poor scarf) and made ready to speak.

"No, the Ghost Goblins will not be disqualified for *smashing my beloved coffin to smithereens!*" He sniffed. There was a moment's silence while he cast a cold eye around the group. He sighed. "Overall I would say it was a very impressive display from *both* teams," he said, nodding slowly. "Not sure I've heard Stone Goblins scream like that before!

"But I'm afraid to say the Ghost Goblins will be disqualified … for cheating!"

Everybody gasped.

"It is clear to me," said Cold Jack, "that you have met with the Bone Collector. How else would you have known how to knit cobwebs, Gusset?"

"HOOZA!" cried the Windy Nibblers. They fizzled and crackled and twisted and turned in the air.

There was a rustle from the shadows and out

stepped the Bone Collector.

"It is true," she said, "that I gave these new ghosts of yours a lesson or two, I'll not deny it. But what about them Windy Nibblers?"

"We never done no cheating!" cried Butt-knuckle.

"Not us, no not never!" cried Armpit.

"Um … yeah!" said Hollowsocket.

"Well, someone created the fog that hid the Stone Goblins at the crucial time. It had 'homemade' written all over it!" said the Bone Collector.

The Windy Nibblers started to look uncomfortable.

"Not us!" shrugged Armpit, weakly.

"Well, if that's true, you won't mind turning out your pockets," said the troll.

The Windy Nibblers shuffled and fidgeted and suddenly became very interested in something on the ground.

Cold Jack narrowed his eyes. "Pockets, empty, now!" he said.

There was a clatter as a handful of fog tablets fell to the floor.

"I *knew* it!" snarled Drysniff, but Cold Jack held up a hand in silence.

"Butt-knuckle," he said, his voice dangerously

low again, "I didn't see you empty your pant pockets!"

"Ain't nothing in there but my botty!" Butt-knuckle mumbled.

Armpit leaned over. "Go on," he said, "let's just get it over with." He grabbed Butt-knuckle's pant elastic and *twanged*.

A small hot water-bottle dropped to the floor with a slosh! It had a pink fluffy cover on it.

Everybody gasped again.

Butt-knuckle flushed.

Cold Jack glared. "What, may I ask, is that?" he said, waggling a finger.

Butt-knuckle caught the glint in Cold Jack's eye and sagged.

"Oh, all right," he said weakly. "Well, the

thing is, my botty gets cold when we sit around on the cold floor, goes all numb it does, and my old mum always said you should never …" he looked up and coughed, "… yeah, well, I like to have something warm to sit on, is all."

"Is that why you been wearing them pants?" asked Hollowsocket. "To hide that hot water bottle?"

Butt-knuckle sagged a little more and nodded miserably. **"Yooou fibber!"** said Armpit again. "And you told us you had to wear them so that everyone could see which one of us was the boss. No wonder you wouldn't give us a turn!"

"Aw, c'mon lads, I'm sorry. Why don't we all—"

Hollowsocket and Armpit were furious. They had both wanted their own pants for ages!

Cold Jack coughed. "Clearly there has been cheating on both sides. So I need to decide exactly what to do."

The Bone Collector did some coughing of her own and stepped forward.

"How about they toss for it?" she said, offering an odd-looking bone. "Heads ... or tails?"

Home Sweet Home

"So what's that – heads or tails?" Cold Jack snapped.

The Bone Collector shrugged. "A bit of both, I reckon, which means I choose!" She picked up the bone and dropped it in her pocket. Cold Jack thought he saw it move.

"Then who wins?" asked Cold Jack, who was beginning to worry this might roll into a third night of arguments and complaints. He really was very tired.

"How about I show Gusset here how to knit three pairs of toasty warm cobweb pants and maybe," she said, looking round at the Windy Nibblers, "just maybe, we might all be able to come to some kind of arrangement ..."

Cold Jack and the Ghost Goblins watched as the Windy Nibblers twittered and crackled with excitement in the thinning fog.

"Look, they've got a little pocket on the inside!" said Armpit.

"And here, see the hot water bottle cover on a string so we don't lose it while we're a-haunting!" said Hollowsocket.

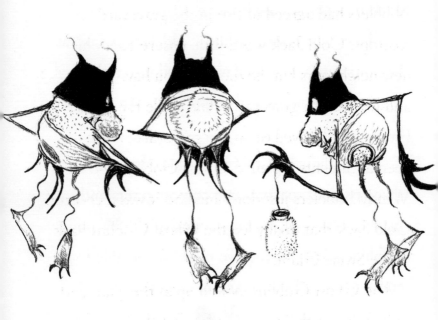

Butt-knuckle, who was relieved they hadn't thrown him out of the gang, smiled. He'd decided to keep his own pants, although he had asked Gusset to sew in a little pocket. "That way, me hot water bottle can fit inside so it doesn't slip about. It'll be all spongy-soft when I go about sitting on them pointy rocks."

In exchange for their new pants, the Windy Nibblers had agreed to live in the graveyard treetops. Cold Jack was a little unsure about his new neighbours but, he thought, you have to live and let live in a graveyard! And while the Ghost Goblins had stayed on in the graveyard, there had been arguments a-plenty. Ghost Goblins and Windy Nibblers just don't mix! So it was a cheerful Cold Jack that finally led the Ghost Goblins back to the Stone Giant.

The Ghost Goblins looked up at the giant and smiled. It was theirs now and at last they were beginning to feel comfortable with who they were – Ghost Goblins and proud of it!

What you have just read is only the beginning for Sludge, Drysniff and Gusset as Ghost Goblins.

Perhaps we will be able to visit them again. Or perhaps they will pay you a visit!

Oh, and the flying pig? Well, much to everyone's surprise she wanted to stay with Cold

Jack. When he arrived back at the graveyard there was a brand-new coffin waiting for him – shiny wheels and everything! The pig took to sitting over the open grave, much like a bird on a nest. Cold Jack was delighted. He was a lot warmer (the pig kept out those winter draughts, which helped his aching bones). His nose dribbles also disappeared.

Except, of course, when night's foggy breath came wafting by.

Please note: No Stone Goblin was harmed during the writing of this story, although Seepage suffered a small bruise on his left elbow which Saggypant accidentally kicked during the running-away scene.

Afterword

Just because you can't see a Ghost Goblin, that doesn't mean they're not there. You have to learn to use your other senses. You may *feel* them creeping across your carpet, you may *smell* that ghastly odour. But it is most likely that you will *hear* them. The jangle of keys, the wail of a cat or the *tap, tap, tapping* of a nodding branch against your bedroom window *could* be ordinary noises outside your house. But then again …

ENJOYED THIS BOOK?

Find out about the other books in the

GOBLINS

series from the website

www.hiddengoblins.co.uk

You can learn about the different characters,
download and print off fun activities
and games, and discover more about
the author, David Melling.

See you there!

stone GOBLINS

tree GOBLINS

puddle GOBLINS

shadow GOBLINS

ghost GOBLINS

Can you think of any other kinds of goblin?

David Melling would love to know about your ideas.

Send us a drawing or painting of your goblin,
and tell us his or her name.

As well as seeing your picture up on the
goblins website, you could win a fantastic
goblin goody bag.

We will choose two winners per month.

Send your drawing to:
Goblins Drawing Competition

UK Readers:
Hodder Children's Books
338 Euston Road
London NW1 3BH

Australian Readers:
Hachette Children's Books
Level 17/207 Kent Street
Sydney NSW 2000

New Zealand Readers:
Hachette Livre NZ Ltd
PO Box 100 749
North Shore City 0745